the CRitter club

Marion Takes a Break

Amy Meets Her Stepsister

Liz at Marigold Lake

by Callie Barkley 💜 illustrated by Marsha Riti

LITTLE SIMON

New York   London   Toronto   Sydney   New Delhi

LITTLE SIMON

An imprint of Simon & Schuster Children's Publishing Division

1230 Avenue of the Americas, New York, New York 10020

Copyright © 2013, 2014 by Simon & Schuster, Inc.

This Little Simon bind-up edition May 2015

All rights reserved, including the right of reproduction in whole or in part in any form. LITTLE SIMON is a registered trademark of Simon & Schuster, Inc., and associated colophon is a trademark of Simon & Schuster, Inc. For information about special discounts for bulk purchases, please contact Simon & Schuster Special Sales at 1-866-506-1949 or business@simonandschuster.com. The Simon & Schuster Speakers Bureau can bring authors to your live event. For more information or to book an event contact the Simon & Schuster Speakers Bureau at 1-866-248-3049 or visit our website at www.simonspeakers.com.

Designed by Laura Roode

Manufactured in the United States of America 0415 FFG

10 9 8 7 6 5 4 3 2 1

ISBN 978-1-4814-5640-1

Table of Contents

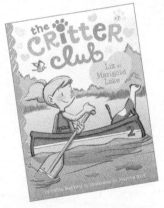

the CRiTTeR club

Marion Takes a Break

Table of Contents

Chapter 1

Too Much to Do

In the school cafeteria Marion saw Amy, Ellie, and Liz sitting near the window. Marion hurried over. She hoped she would have time to eat her lunch. The recess bell was going to ring in just ten minutes!

"What took you so long?" Amy asked. She scooted down the bench to make space for Marion.

"I couldn't find my lunch!" Marion said, sitting down. "I thought it was in my cubby, but it was actually in my backpack under my ballet shoes and leotard."

I've got to get organized! Marion thought as she started to eat. *Better add that to my to-do list!*

Marion was good at making lists. It helped to keep her busy life in order. Now that it was fall, Marion was busier than ever! She worked very hard in school and always got perfect grades. She also had piano lessons and ballet class every week.

Then there was her horse, Coco. Marion went to the stables at least three times a week. Having a horse was a lot of work, but Marion loved every bit of it.

"So what were you talking about?" Marion asked. She took a big bite of her sandwich.

"The kittens!" Ellie exclaimed. There was a new litter of kittens at The Critter Club, the animal shelter that the four girls helped run in their friend Ms. Sullivan's barn. The girls had met Ms. Sullivan when they found her lost puppy, Rufus.

After that, Ms. Sullivan decided

the town needed an animal shelter. She had an empty barn; Amy's mom, Dr. Purvis, had a lot of advice to offer since she was a veterinarian; and the girls had lots of energy—plus a love of animals.

So The Critter Club began! Since then the girls had helped bunnies and a turtle. They had even done pet sitting over the summer. Now it was up to them to find homes for an entire litter of kittens!

The kittens' mother was a stray cat. When a teacher found them all behind the school, she brought them to the vet clinic. Dr. Purvis had suggested that the five healthy kittens stay at The

Critter Club, and the girls were very excited to help take care of them!

"The mother cat and one kitten are still at the clinic," Amy told her friends. "My mom said that the mama cat needs more rest. And even though the tabby kitten's injured paw is getting better, he still needs to heal for a while longer too."

The girls took turns helping out at The Critter Club after school and on weekends. "Liz and I had such a great time at the club yesterday afternoon. Those kittens are just so cute!" Ellie squealed.

"That's the thing," Amy said, "it should be easy to find homes for them. I was thinking . . . what if we have a big party at The Critter Club? People could come meet the kittens!"

Marion, Ellie, and Liz all nodded. "That's a great idea!" said

Liz. "Everyone would see how cute they are!"

"We could have music!" Ellie suggested. She loved to perform. "I could sing!"

"We could get dressed up!" Marion added. She had a silver dress that would be perfect.

"We could put up pretty lights—and some artwork!" said Liz. She was an amazing artist.

Marion imagined how wonderful Liz's paintings would look hanging around The Critter Club. They would really jazz up the barn!

Just then the recess bell rang. Marion chewed fast, trying to finish her sandwich. Then the four friends headed outside. It was autumn in Santa Vista, but in their part of California, it never got too cold.

Amy walked next to Marion. "Maybe we'll think of more party

ideas this afternoon," said Amy.

"This afternoon?" Marion mumbled. Her mouth was still full.

"Yeah, at The Critter Club?" Amy said. "It's Monday—our day to help out. Remember?"

Marion had forgotten! It wasn't like her to get her schedule mixed up. "Uh? The Critter Club? Of course I will be there!"

Chapter 2

Marion Makes a Mess

If we finish early, I'll have time to ride Coco before dinner, Marion was thinking.

"Marion, I think you fed that kitten already," Amy was saying.

Marion looked down. The light gray kitten wasn't drinking. He didn't seem interested in Marion's bottle of milk. "Oh! You're right!"

Marion exclaimed. "What am I doing?"

She and Amy were at The Critter Club, feeding the tiny kittens.

Dr. Purvis had told them that the kittens were only about five weeks old! Feeding such young cats was tricky. Luckily, Dr. Purvis had shown the girls just what to do. She

had even made them a poster to remind them of the steps.

♡ How to Feed the Kittens ♡

Step 1: Take out one container marked "Kitten Milk" from the refrigerator. This is special milk that is just like their mother's.

Step 2: Pour the milk into a clean baby bottle.

Step 3: Warm the bottle in the bottle warmer until light turns green.

Step 4: Hold kitten, sitting up, in your lap, or let kitten lie on his/her belly while eating. Do not cradle kitten belly up like a baby.

Marion and Amy had come to
the club right after school. Marion
had been rushing around ever
since. She really wanted to get to
the stables to ride Coco. They had a
big competition coming up. Marion
and Coco had won it last year, and

Marion had her sights on taking the blue ribbon again this year. There was a good reason blue was her favorite color!

The only thing was, they would need some extra practice if they wanted to win.

Marion warmed a bottle for the black kitten. But hurrying across the barn, she dropped it on the barn floor and had to make up a new one. Then she knocked over the bottle warmer, spilling the water inside. Next, Marion didn't screw a bottle top on tight enough. Some milk spilled on the white kitten.

"Oh, for goodness' sake!" she cried. "I just can't do anything right!"

Amy came over. "Marion, are you okay?" Amy asked kindly. "You don't seem like yourself."

She's right, thought Marion. *I'm not myself. I never, ever mess up this*

much! Marion was used to getting things right the first time.

She sighed and wiped up the milk. "I'm fine," she said. "Just in a rush!" She looked up at Amy. "I need to get to the stables before dinner. We have a competition coming up,

and Coco and I need some extra practice."

Amy smiled. "Oh, I get it now," she said. "Well, I can finish up here if you need to go."

Marion studied Amy's face. "Really?" Marion asked. "Are you sure?"

Amy looked around. "We're almost done anyway," she said. "Really! You should go. Say hi to Coco for me!"

Marion felt so lucky to have such a great best friend. She gave Amy a huge hug. "Thank you!" she said as she turned to go. "You are the best!"

Chapter 13

One Wrong Step

That afternoon Marion rode Coco until the sun started to set.

The next day, Tuesday, she headed to the stables right after school. She and Coco worked on walk, trot, canter, and gallop all afternoon.

Then on Wednesday afternoon Marion had her riding lesson. She and her teacher worked on some low jumps.

By Thursday Marion was starting to feel ready. "We've got two more weeks, Coco," she said to her pretty brown horse. Marion was brushing Coco in her stall. "Two weeks until the show. I know we can do it."

She looked over at the stall door. Coco's

ribbons hung in a row.
"We'll get you another
blue ribbon to hang up!"

Marion said good-bye
to Coco before heading
to the changing room. She *loved*
her riding outfit—her tall boots,
her breeches, her crisp, navy blue
jacket, but Marion also loved what
she'd worn to school that day. It was
her *favorite fall outfit*: her corduroy
skirt, lavender cardigan, purple

tights, and purple flats. She was excited to put them back on!

"Marion!" a voice called from outside her dressing cubby. "Are you there?" Marion knew that voice. It was her six-year-old sister, Gabby. She took riding lessons at the stable too. Gabby was going to compete in the junior division at the horse show. "Come on! Mom and I are waiting in the car!"

"Uh, I'm coming!" Marion called. She hurried to pull on

her tights, but pulling on tights fast was very hard to do. Marion stepped into her flats and hurried outside. She saw her mom's car by the corral fence. Marion ran across the stable yard.

Halfway there she stepped in a dip in the gravel path. Her left foot twisted in a strange way when she landed.

"Ow!" Marion cried. She felt a sharp pain in her ankle. Her leg gave out and she fell onto the gravel. "Ow! My ankle!" It felt so weird—and hurt *so much!*

When Marion didn't get up, Marion's mom and sister ran over from the car.

What happened next was a big blur. Marion's mom and sister helped her up, but she couldn't walk. Standing on her ankle hurt

way too much so Marion's mom gave her a piggyback ride to the car. They drove straight to the hospital, where Marion's dad, a doctor, met them in the emergency room.

Dr. Ballard examined her ankle and ordered an X-ray. Marion began to worry.

Before long, Marion's dad put

his hand on her shoulder. He held the X-ray up to the light.

"Bad news, kiddo. It looks like you have a pretty bad sprain," he said. "You're going to need a cast."

"A *cast*?" Marion was shocked. "For how long?"

"At least three weeks—maybe four," her dad said. "You'll have crutches to help you get around, but you will need to take it easy for a while. But guess what? Casts come in all kinds of cool colors!"

For once Marion didn't care about fashion. She couldn't believe

what she was hearing. This *wasn't* happening! "No, no, no! I can't be in a cast for three weeks! Dad, the horse show is in *two weeks*!"

Her dad put down the X-ray. He

took Marion's hand. "I'm really sorry, honey," he said. "It's going to take time for your ankle to heal." He sighed a big sigh. "I'm afraid the horse show is out."

Chapter 4

Friends to the Rescue!

Marion closed her book and tossed it onto the sofa. She just *couldn't* concentrate.

It was Friday afternoon. She'd had the cast less than twenty-four hours, and already she was tired of it. She had missed school because she wasn't used to walking with the crutches yet.

"By Monday you'll be a pro," her dad had said that morning. "Then you can try them at school."

Monday couldn't come soon enough for Marion. *I'm missing everything!* she thought. *I can't go to ballet next week. I can't ride Coco. I don't even know what's going on in math class!*

Marion's mom was home with her, so Marion's dad picked up Gabby from her riding lesson at the stables. She walked in with her riding clothes still on. Marion

couldn't help feeling envious.

What's worse than not being able to ride in the horse show? she asked herself. *Having a sister who is riding in the horse show.* Marion knew it wasn't her sister's fault. Still, it was going to be *so* hard to watch Gabby ride when Marion couldn't.

Just then the doorbell rang. Marion heard her mom open the front door. Moments later Amy, Ellie, and Liz poked their heads in to the family room. "Can we come in?" Amy asked.

"*Yes!*" Marion cried. She was so glad to see her friends.

Ellie handed Marion a very pretty bouquet of flowers. "At school Mrs. Sienna told the class about your ankle!" Ellie said.

"We had to come see you," added Liz. She gave Marion a get-well card she had made.

"We thought you might need cheering up," said Amy. "Oh, and these." She handed Marion a tin. Marion opened the lid. Inside were Amy's mother's famous oatmeal raisin cookies. They were Marion's favorite.

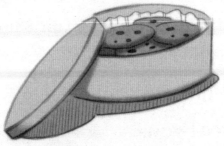

Marion forced a smile. "Thanks, guys," she said. She put the flowers, the card, and the cookies next to her on the coffee table.

"Wait," said Amy. "Aren't you going to have a cookie?"

Marion shrugged. "Not right now," she said with a big sigh. "I'm not hungry."

Amy looked at Ellie and Liz. "Uh-oh," Amy said. "Not hungry for her favorite cookies? She *does* need to be cheered up."

Ellie giggled. "Well, then, let's tell her," she said. "Listen, Marion. About the sleepover tonight—"

Marion slapped her forehead as it hit her. "The sleepover!" she cried. "Today is Friday! I forgot!"

The four girls had a sleepover almost every Friday night. They each took turns hosting. Marion knew that this week it was at Liz's house.

"Oh," she groaned, *"another thing I can't do!"* She wasn't feeling up to getting off the sofa—not until she could practice more with her crutches.

"Yeah," said Amy. "We thought you might not be able to come to Liz's."

"So we brought the sleepover to you!" said Liz.

Marion gasped. "Really?" she said. "You mean we can have it here instead?"

"Sure!" Liz said. "I'll host next week instead. Now, you've got to let me sign your cast!"

"Ooh! Me too!" said Amy.

"Me three!" said Ellie.

"Sure!" Marion said. Then she smiled—for real this time.

Chapter 5

Back to School?

On Monday morning Marion woke up feeling excited. After practicing with her crutches all weekend, her mom and dad had agreed she could go back to school!

Marion hopped on her good foot to her closet. She wanted to pick out the perfect outfit.

Then she realized something.

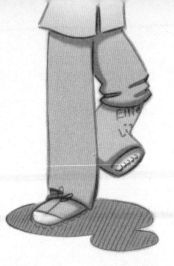

She couldn't wear tights or leggings. They wouldn't fit over her cast. And—Marion gasped—she could only wear one shoe!

None of my favorite outfits will look as good with this cast! she thought.

Marion had to wear her least favorite jeans. And for her one shoe, her mom wanted her to wear a sneaker. "Comfort and grip. That's what you need!" Mrs. Ballard said.

Marion checked her outfit in the mirror. "This day is not off to a good start," she said grumpily.

At school things didn't get much better. It took her forever to get from the drop-off circle to her classroom. She was the last one in her seat. Marion hated being last.

In gym class Marion couldn't play kickball. She had to sit on the bench and watch. Amy, Liz, and Ellie took turns keeping her company.

At lunchtime Marion couldn't carry her lunchbox *and* walk on crutches at the same time. Amy was happy to carry her lunch for her, but Marion didn't like the feeling of not being able to do things on her own.

As the week went on, Marion got more frustrated. At her piano lesson her cast made it hard to use the foot pedal. None of Marion's songs sounded right.

At ballet class, all the students were learning new moves. Marion went so she could at least see the steps. But she couldn't practice them. *Wow, everyone looks so graceful,* she thought. She wished she were up there, right in front.

Hardest of all was visiting Coco. The stables were very busy with riders getting ready for the horse show.

Marion fed Coco a carrot and brushed her mane. "I'm so sorry, Coco," she whispered. "You have worked so hard to win. I'm just a huge failure—at everything."

Chapter 6

Broken Dreams

Finally it was Thursday—Marion's and Amy's turn after school at The Critter Club. *At last!* thought Marion. *Feeding the little kittens is something fun that even I can do with this cast!*

It turned out this wasn't exactly true. Marion couldn't get around on crutches while holding a kitten in her arms. And she definitely couldn't get around with a kitten *and* a bottle.

"That's okay," said Amy. "We'll feed them together. You hold this one. I'll get the bottle."

That's when Marion's frustration bubbled over. "I can't do anything right!" she burst out. Tears rolled down her cheeks. "I took one wrong step, and now my ankle is sprained! This cast will be on for weeks. And everything keeps on going without me! I'll never be able to catch up!"

She covered her face with her hands and sobbed. Amy hugged her tight.

"Oh, Marion, it's okay! You're going to be better so soon!" Amy said. "You make it sound like

everything is a big race, but it isn't. You don't have to be number one all the time."

Amy let go of Marion. She looked her right in the eye. "You know, we all love you for *you*," Amy said. "It's not because you get awesome grades, or

play piano amazingly . . . or dance like a pro . . . or win blue ribbons with Coco. Should I keep going?"

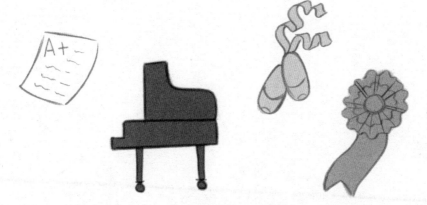

Marion laughed through her tears. "No, that's okay," she said.

Amy smiled. "It must be really hard not to be able to do your favorite things, but maybe, for now, just think of the things you *can* do."

Amy looked down at the kittens. "Like feed these fuzz balls."

Marion wiped her tears. She took a deep breath. "You're right," she said with a smile. "Thanks, Amy."

Then, the girls fed the kittens—together.

Chapter 7

The Plan

The next day at school Amy had great news.

"Mom says the kitten with the injured paw is doing much better!" she told the girls at lunch. "He can go home—well, he could if he had a home."

"Yeah," said Liz. "Too bad none of the kittens have been adopted.

Hey! He could come stay at The Critter Club too, right?"

"Great idea, Liz!" Ellie said.

Amy nodded. "He might need some special care for a little while, but we can handle that. Right?"

"Right!" the others chimed in.

"And while he gets stronger," said Marion, "we can work on finding homes for *all* the kittens!"

Marion was feeling more like

her old self again. Her talk with Amy had helped a lot. She got out a notebook and pen to start a to-do list.

"So what about Amy's idea?" Marion asked. "Having a big party at The Critter Club so people can meet the kittens?"

"I still love that idea," said Ellie.

"There's just one thing," said Liz. "Throwing a big party costs money. We'd have to buy food and decorations."

"That's true," Amy agreed. "It could get pretty expensive."

Marion thought it over. How could they get lots of people to meet the kittens? She remembered when they were trying to find homes for

some bunnies. Ellie was starring in the school play. She had gotten the bunnies up on stage.

Could we get the kittens in some kind of show? thought Marion. *A show . . . A show . . .* Then it hit her. *The horse show!*

"I've got it!" Marion exclaimed. "We could bring the kittens to the big horse show next weekend! We

could set up a booth. There will be lots of kids and parents there!"

"Yes!" said Amy. "Marion, that's a *great* idea. Maybe my mom could bake some cookies for us to give away to people so they stop by the booth!"

"I could bring my karaoke machine!" Ellie chimed in.

"Ellie," began Liz, "you are a *fantastic* singer, but—"

"Oh no!" Ellie said. "Not so I can sing. We

could use the microphone to get people's attention."

Liz giggled. "Oh! That makes sense. And I can be in charge of decorating the booth."

Suddenly Marion knew what *she* wanted to be in charge of. "Can I make a special collar for each kitten?" she asked. "That way they'll each look their best for the big day."

The girls agreed it was a plan—a *great* plan!

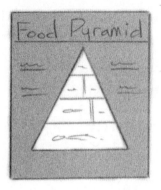

79

Chapter 8

The Sixth Kitten

Marion lined up the kittens' collars she had made so far. "Five down, one to go!" she said.

She was at The Critter Club with Amy, Ellie, and Liz. All four had been spending extra time there. The horse show was only three days away, and there was a lot they wanted to get organized.

"Wow, Marion! Those are all so pretty!" Ellie said.

"Thanks!" Marion replied. She had worked hard on her creations. She had thought a lot about which color would look best on each kitten. "The braided green one is for the little black kitten," Marion explained. "The bright purple satin collar is for the white kitten. The red velvet will look great

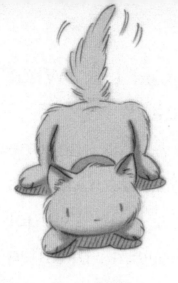

on the black and white kitten, and the pink collar will really stand out on the silver kitten. The sunny yellow collar goes on the dark gray kitten." *Whew!* Marion took a breath.

"Great colors!" said Liz. "What about the tabby kitten?"

The tabby kitten was the one with the healing paw. Marion was saving his collar for last. "I've got something extraspecial planned for Ollie," Marion said with a smile.

The name had been Marion's suggestion. All the girls gave Ollie extra care and cuddles, but Marion had a special place in her heart for him. His brothers and sisters could now run and jump and play. But poor Ollie was still limping around a little. He would often sit off to the side and watch the others.

Sometimes Marion felt like she and Ollie were going through the same thing.

Marion reached for her clipboard. She checked the list. "So what's left to do before Saturday?" she asked.

"Mom and I are baking another batch of cookies tonight," said Amy. "We've got six dozen so far! We're going to bring a big cooler of lemonade, too."

"Great!" said Marion, making a note on her list. "Food, check!"

"And I've got almost all of the

decorations ready," said Liz. "I'm still making some really long paper chains in bright colors. We can hang them all around the sides of our table. Tonight I'll make the sign!"

"And Mom helped me put new batteries in my karaoke

machine," Ellie added. "Now I'm thinking up catchy things to say at the horse show. What do you think of this?" Ellie held an imaginary microphone to her mouth. *"Kittens and cookies! Cookies and kittens!"* she boomed.

The girls laughed at Ellie's announcer voice. "That will get people's attention, all right!" Amy said.

Marion checked things off on the list. "Decorations, check! Karaoke machine, check!"

There was one other thing Marion wondered about. "Guys, how will we know who *should* adopt a kitten—who would give them a good home?" Marion wanted to make sure the kittens would be taken care of.

"Good thinking, Marion," Amy said. "My mom will be there the whole time, so she can talk to people about having kittens as pets."

Marion nodded. She knew that

Dr. Purvis would make sure the kittens went to loving families.

She hated the idea of any of the kittens living somewhere they wouldn't be loved . . . especially little Ollie.

Chapter 9

Kittens and Cookies

"Wow!" said Liz, leaning close to Marion. "There are a lot of people here!" She had to speak up. Right next to them Ellie was half talking, half singing into the karaoke machine microphone. She couldn't quite contain her musical side.

"Kittens and cookies! Come have a looksie!"

"Lots of people *and* lots of horses!" Marion replied to Liz.

The horse show was being held at the Santa Vista fairgrounds—near Ms. Sullivan's house. There were two big performance rings, and stands for people to sit and watch. The parking lot was full of cars and horse trailers.

The girls and their parents had come early. They had picked a shady spot, between the parking lot and the performance area, where they had set up the booth. It was made out of Marion's family's beach

The Critter Club Presents: "Meet the Kittens!"

umbrella and Liz's family's big folding table. With Liz's decorations and sign, the girls thought it looked great!

The kittens were playing happily in a little fenced area behind the table. Ms. Sullivan had brought them over from The Critter Club.

Earlier Marion had put on their special new collars.

"They all look sooo cute!" Ellie squealed. "And I love Ollie's collar, Marion."

Marion liked it too. It was a sparkly silver ribbon with a heart charm on the front. The other girls couldn't see, but on the back of the charm was a message.

To OLLIE, LOVE ALWAYS, MARION.

It had already been a busy morning! Lots of people were stopping by the booth. Some just stopped by for cookies and lemonade, but many others asked Dr. Purvis about adopting a kitten. Amy's mom was chatting nonstop!

Right before noon Marion took a

break. It was almost Gabby's turn in the ring! She went with her mom and dad to watch from the stands. It *was* hard to watch her sister ride, but not because she was jealous. She was nervous and *excited* for her little sister!

As Gabby did her routine, Marion was amazed—her sister was great! When Gabby finished, Marion cheered louder than anyone.

Back at The Critter Club booth,

Marion could hardly wait to tell her friends.

"She and her horse both looked so calm. Their walk, trot, canter, and gallop was the best I've seen them do!" Then Marion noticed that there were only three kittens in the little play area. "What happened to the black, the white, and the silver kittens?"

Dr. Purvis smiled. "Three of the families from this morning came back," she said. "They wanted to adopt. I'm sure they will give our little friends great homes!"

Marion smiled happily. Secretly, though, she was glad none of the families had chosen Ollie. She would have been sad to have missed saying good-bye.

The hours sped by. More people stopped by the booth. One by one the cookies disappeared and the lemonade cooler got emptier. Ellie's voice had gotten tired, too, and she had turned off the karaoke machine.

The Critter Club Presents,
Meet the Kittens!

Before Marion knew it, two more kittens had been adopted—Ollie was the only one left.

The horse show was almost done. The loudspeaker came on, and Marion could hear a voice reading a list of winners. *Last year they read my name,* she thought sadly. *Not this year.*

Just then Marion *did* hear her

name announced!

"The junior division blue ribbon goes to rider number fourteen, Ballard." That was Marion's last name! Then the announcer went on: "Congratulations to Gabby Ballard!"

Marion gasped and clapped. Her sister had won a blue ribbon!

Surprise!

What a day! The girls had found homes for five kittens *and* Gabby had won!

"I'm so proud of you!" Marion said to her little sister. She gave Gabby a great big hug. At that moment seeing her sister win was even better than getting her own blue ribbon!

"Let's celebrate!" said Marion's mom. She invited all the girls, their parents, and Ms. Sullivan back to their house for dinner.

Together everyone packed up the booth. It took Marion's dad a few extra minutes to get the umbrella back in their car. Then Marion and Gabby and their parents were on their way home—with Ollie. He sat, all alone, in a cat carrier at Marion's feet.

"Don't worry, Ollie, we'll find you a home," she said to him.

The Ballards were the last to

arrive at their own house. Marion's dad and sister took Ollie inside. Marion's mom got the crutches from the trunk. She helped Marion out of the car and up the walk.

When Marion hopped through
the front door, she couldn't believe
her eyes. There were balloons
everywhere! There was a big cake on
the coffee table. A colorful banner
hung over the fireplace.

"Surprise!" everyone shouted. There was Amy, Liz, Ellie, and their parents; Liz's big brother, Stewart; Ellie's little brother, Toby; Ellie's nana Gloria; Ms. Sullivan; and Rufus, too! They were all looking at Marion!

"A party . . . for *me?*" Marion asked in shock. "But Gabby is the one who won."

Marion's mom gave Gabby a squeeze. "Yes, but now it's a party for you *and* Gabby!" she said. "We're very proud of you *both*, Marion."

Marion's dad put an arm around

her shoulders. "We know nothing has been easy with the cast," he said. "Missing the horse show was really tough, but you made the best of it. You put your efforts into working hard for The Critter Club."

He looked around at the girls. "All of you did . . . and it really paid off."

Marion felt great. Actually, she felt better than great. She felt *proud*. She hadn't won anything or gotten a perfect grade. Instead, she knew she had done an important job. "Finding homes for five kittens in one day *is* pretty awesome!" she said happily.

"You can make that six," said Marion's mom. She was holding Ollie.

Marion's smile disappeared from her face. "Six?" she said. "Has . . . has Ollie been adopted too?" Marion prepared for the bad news.

"Yep!" her mom said. "He's been adopted by . . ."

"*Us!*" said Marion's dad and sister together.

Marion's eyes went wide. One of her crutches fell over. She almost lost her balance but didn't. "Do you mean it?" she cried. "Really? Really, *really*?"

Marion's mom and dad smiled. "We really mean it," her dad said. "But there's one other person who has to agree."

Marion looked around in surprise. "Who?" she asked.

Her parents glanced over at Dr. Purvis.

"I can't think of a better home for little Ollie," Dr. Purvis said with a smile.

As Marion sat down on the couch, her mother handed Ollie to her. The rest of the girls gathered around Marion and hugged her and the adorable kitten.

"As soon as my ankle is all better, we're going to have lots of adventures together, Ollie!" Marion told the kitten.

Ollie purred and nestled happily into Marion's lap.

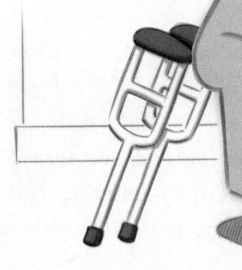

121

the CRITTER club

Amy Meets Her Stepsister

Table of Contents

Chapter 1

Big, Exciting News!

Amy Purvis's mom grabbed a pot-holder. She lifted the pot lid. Amy took a sniff.

"Mmmm," Amy said. "That smells *so* good!"

Inside the pot was a big batch of their famous chicken noodle soup. They had made it together. "The perfect dinner for a cool night,"

Amy's mom said with a smile.

Amy giggled. "Mom, this batch will last us all year!" It *was* a lot of soup for just the two of them.

Amy set the table. She put out two napkins and two soup spoons. Meanwhile, Amy's mom ladled soup into bowls.

Just as they sat down to eat, the phone rang.

"Start without me!" said Amy's mom, popping up to answer it.

Amy slurped up some broth and noodles. Right away, she felt warm all over.

"Oh, hi, Eliot!" she heard her mom say into the phone.

Amy's face lit up. Eliot was her father. He lived in Orange Blossom, a big town near Santa Vista. Even though her parents were divorced,

Amy got to see her dad a lot.

"Uh-huh," her mom was saying into the phone. "I bet she would love that!" She looked over at Amy and smiled. "Why don't you ask her?" Her mom held out the phone to Amy. "Your dad has a question for you," she said.

Amy jumped up and took the phone.

"Hi, Dad!" she said excitedly. "What's up?"

"Hey, kiddo," came her dad's voice through the phone. "How would you like to spend this weekend at my house?"

"Really?" said Amy. She loved her weekends with her dad. "But I thought that was *next* weekend."

"I know," her dad said. "But I've got some really big and exciting news to tell you."

News? "What is it?" Amy asked.

"You know what? I want to tell you in person," her dad said. "Oh! And Julia is going to come visit on Saturday too."

Julia was Amy's dad's girlfriend. He had met her about a year ago. Amy really liked Julia. She still kind of wished her mom and dad were married. But since *they* didn't want that, Amy was happy her dad had

met someone as nice as Julia.

"So I'll pick you up tomorrow. Okay?" her dad said.

"Okay! Bye!" said Amy, and she hung up the phone. She was so glad she wouldn't have to wait too long for the weekend. Tomorrow was Friday!

Then it hit her. *Friday.* It was sleepover night with her three best friends: Marion, Ellie, and Liz. They had one almost every week.

With a pang of disappointment, Amy flopped down into her

chair. "Oh, no. This means I can't go to the sleepover at Marion's."

Amy's mom patted her on the back. "You'll have fun with your dad, sweetie. And when we host

next week's sleepover, we can make it extra special."

Amy nodded. *And besides,* she thought, *we have lots of sleepovers. But how often does Dad have big, exciting news?*

Now she was really curious. What *was* the big news?

Chapter 2

A Lunchtime Mystery

Amy couldn't wait for school the next day. She wanted to tell her friends about her weekend with her dad—and the mystery news! Lunchtime was their first chance to talk.

"Maybe your dad is going to run for president!" Ellie said excitedly. Her brown eyes twinkled. "Or he is

going to Hollywood to be in movies!
Or he found out you're related to the
Queen of England!"

Amy giggled. Ellie just loved the
idea of being famous!

Marion slurped the last of her

chocolate milk. "Maybe he will take you on a shopping spree!" she suggested.

Then Liz spoke up. "Maybe your dad wants to write about The Critter Club in his newspaper!"

The Coastal County Courier

The Critter Club!

Hmmm . . . , thought Amy. That was a possibility. Amy's dad was the editor of a newspaper called *The Coastal County Courier.* He knew all about The Critter Club. It was the animal shelter that the girls ran in their friend Ms. Sullivan's barn.

"That could be it," said Amy. "My dad did say one time that it would make a good story—how the club got started."

And it actually *was* a good story. Before the four girls really knew Ms. Marge Sullivan, they had helped her find her missing

puppy, Rufus. Then Ms. Sullivan had a great idea. She decided Santa Vista needed an animal shelter to help lost and stray animals. Ms. Sullivan had an empty barn, and the girls had a love of animals, and that's how it all began!

The Critter Club

It helped that Amy's mom was a veterinarian. Dr. Purvis taught the girls how to take care of the different animals that had been at The Critter Club so far:

bunnies, kittens, dogs— even a turtle and a tarantula!

"Well, I am sorry I won't be around this weekend," Amy said. "I wanted to help out with the eggs."

They were incubating a dozen chicken eggs at The Critter Club.

A local farmer had dropped them off a week before. His family had to move. They had sold or given away most of their farm animals.

Then, before their move, their best hen had laid a clutch of eggs. But she didn't want to sit on them. Amy's mom said sometimes hens did that.

Luckily, the farmer knew about The Critter Club. He had brought the eggs and the incubator. The

girls were so excited to help them hatch. Then they would find the chicks new homes!

"Don't worry," said Liz. "We can handle the eggs. They're not due to hatch for another week."

"But we will miss you at the sleepover tonight!" Marion said. She put an arm around Amy's shoulders.

"Oooh! And call one of us when you get the good news!" Ellie begged. "I can't wait to hear it!"

Chapter 3

Dinner with Dad

The drive from Amy's house to her dad's only took about twenty minutes. But in that time, Amy had asked him the same question ten times.

"*Now* can you tell me the big, exciting news?" she asked again. They were pulling into his driveway.

Her dad shook his head for the

eleventh time. "Nope! You'll have to wait until dinner!" he said. "First let's get you settled in. Then we're going out."

We're going out to dinner? Amy thought. *This* is *a big deal.*

Amy walked into her dad's house, thinking once again how cool it was. The walls were painted bright colors. The furniture was simple and square. Her dad said the style was called "modern." His house

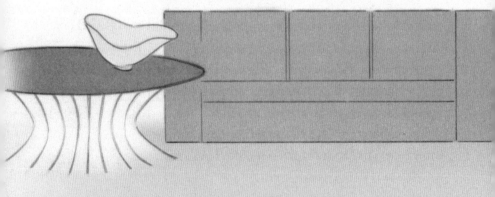

was so different from her mom's house, which was very cozy but not as colorful.

The art on her dad's walls was also really bright. *I've got to bring*

Liz here sometime, Amy thought. Liz was an amazing artist. *Maybe she can tell me what these are.*

Amy loved that she had her very own room at her dad's house. She plopped her heavy backpack down

on her bed. Then she unpacked. She had a huge pile of books. She had brought the newest Nancy Drew mystery, plus *The Wind in the Willows, Black Beauty,* and *The Wonderful Wizard of Oz.*

"Hungry?" her dad asked as he poked his head into Amy's room.

Amy nodded.

So off they went to dinner. It was a short walk to Amy's favorite

restaurant in Orange Blossom—
The Library. The walls were wall-
papered with old book pages. The
menu was Amy's favorite part.

The Library

Starter: The Secret Garden Salad

Appetizer: The Mad Hatter's
           Tea Sandwiches

Entree: 20,000 Leagues Under
        the Seafood Sampler

Amy and her dad ordered. When
the waiter had gone, her dad smiled
across the table.

"I have a pile of old newspapers we can cut up," he told her.

"Cool!" Amy exclaimed.

Amy and her dad loved creating poems together. They cut words out of newspapers or magazines. They moved them around until they had a poem they liked.

Then they glued the words to a piece of paper.

"And, hey! What's going on with The Critter Club?" her dad went on.

Amy told him all about the eggs that were going to hatch. But she really wanted to talk about some-thing else.

"Dad, wasn't there some big news?" Amy said. She looked at him and squinted. "It's dinnertime. Can you tell me *now*?"

Her dad smiled. "Okay, you're

right," he said. "Well, Julia is going to come over tomorrow."

"Right," said Amy. "You told me on the phone." She and her dad and Julia always had fun together.

"And Julia's going to bring some-one with her," her dad went on. "Do you remember that Julia has a daughter? Her name is Chloe."

Amy nodded. She remembered. Julia talked about Chloe a lot. Amy had never met her because Chloe was often away visiting her dad in Arizona. Amy felt the slightest flutter of butterflies in her stomach. Amy was shy about meeting new people. *But Julia is nice*, she thought. *I bet Chloe will be nice too.*

"She's eight years old, just like you are!" her dad continued.

"And . . . here's the really big news: the reason we'd love you and Chloe to finally meet is that Julia and I are engaged!"

Engaged? Amy's face flushed a little. "Like, getting married?" she asked.

Her dad nodded. "That's the idea," he said. "We haven't set a date yet. But we'd like to get married someday—maybe next year."

"Oh," was all Amy could think of to say. Her mind was racing. *If Dad and Julia get married, will Julia be my stepmom? And what about Chloe? Will she be my . . . stepsister?*

Now there were a million butterflies in Amy's stomach. They were fluttering around like crazy. She was really nervous about meeting Chloe.

What if we don't have anything in

common? Amy thought. *What if I don't like her? Or worse: what if she doesn't like me?*

Chapter 4

Chloe

The next morning, Amy woke up to the smell of pancakes. *Yum!* She got out of bed and put on her slippers. As she did, she remembered part of a dream she'd had. In it, she had been getting ready for a big fancy ball. Her dress was perfect. She was all set to leave. Then three mean stepsisters appeared and tore her beautiful dress to shreds.

Stepsisters, Amy thought. *I guess I really am nervous about meeting Chloe!*

Down in the kitchen, her dad was flipping pancakes. There was a place set at the table for Amy. Next to it was a stack of newspapers.

"Breakfast, coming right up!" her dad said. "Have a seat. I wrote you a poem."

Amy found the paper on the table, next to her fork.

MAYBE pigs **fly**, moo?
And maybe birds
But there is no way
someone won't Like you.

Amy giggled. "Thanks, Dad," she said. It was like he could read her mind.

Her dad came over and gave her a kiss on the head. "Don't worry," he said. "You and Chloe will get along great."

Amy had two pancakes—then one more. She and her dad cut and pasted some poems together.

Then Amy went to her room to get dressed.

As she put on her shoes, she heard the doorbell. *Ding-dong!*

Amy took a deep breath. Then she walked toward the front hall.

Her dad was already at the door. At first, Amy could only see Julia on the front stoop. She looked the same as Amy remembered: shiny, straight black hair, sparkling brown eyes, and a big, friendly smile.

"Amy!" Julia said, spotting her. She breezed in and greeted Amy with a hug. "It's so good to see you. And I'm so happy for you to meet Chloe."

Julia stepped aside. Amy realized Chloe was standing right behind Julia. In fact, Chloe was holding on to the back of Julia's blue coat. Then, quickly, Chloe let go. She smiled at Amy.

Amy's first thought was: *She looks so much like her mom!* Chloe had the same shiny dark hair, but hers was in braids.

Her second thought was: *Ellie would love that outfit.* She had on a dark green dress and shiny black patent leather shoes. It reminded Amy of the pretty costumes Ellie liked to wear.

"Hi," said Chloe with a small wave.

"Nice to meet you," Amy said—
and tried hard not to blush. It happened every time Amy felt shy or
embarrassed. And at that moment,
she was feeling both.

Chapter 5

A Messy Beginning

Julia held up a plastic container. "It's not too early for cookies, is it?" she asked, smiling. "I was hoping you girls could help me by decorating them."

Amy thought that sounded fun!

Amy's dad set the girls up at the kitchen table. Julia had made sugar cookies that were shaped like hearts

and stars. There were tubes of icing, sprinkles, and colored sugar. Julia put out a glass of water.

"For smoothing the icing," she explained.

Chloe sat down. Amy took the seat across from her.

"Julia and I are going to do some gardening out back," Amy's dad told the girls.

"Just give us a call if you need

us. Okay?" added Julia.

Chloe smiled at her mom. Amy nodded and took a cookie. Chloe did too.

Then, as their parents went out the back door, both girls reached for the tube of yellow icing.

"Oh!" said Amy. "It's okay. You take it. I'll use the blue."

Chloe didn't say anything. She just took the yellow. Then she scooted her chair a little farther from the table.

Why did she do that? Amy wondered. *Maybe she just needs more room to decorate. . . .*

She glanced over at Chloe. Chloe had her eyes locked on her cookie. For a few minutes, the kitchen was silent.

Is it possible? thought Amy. *Someone who's even shyer than I am?*

As shy as she was herself, Amy wanted to be a good hostess. "So, what school do you go to?" she asked Chloe.

At first, Chloe didn't answer. She was still staring at her cookie, squeezing out the yellow icing. But then she blurted out: "Orange Blossom School for Girls."

"Oh," said Amy. "I know where that is." She waited to see if Chloe had more to say.

She didn't.

So Amy said, "I go to Santa Vista Elementary."

Chloe didn't look up.

"My three best friends and I started an animal shelter," Amy went on. "It's called The Critter Club. We take care of strays and lost or hurt animals."

Chloe still didn't say anything.

"Do you like animals?" Amy tried.

For the first time since their parents had left, Chloe looked up. *"Ew,"* she said. Her face scrunched up, like she smelled something gross. "Animals are dirty and smelly. Why would you want to be around them so much?"

Amy felt her cheeks flush hot. She had no idea what to say to that.

Just then, Chloe reached for the pink icing. Her elbow knocked over the water glass. Water spilled onto the cookie plate, soaking the cookies.

Quickly Amy reached for a towel. "Oh, don't worry," Amy said. "It's not a big deal."

Then Amy's dad walked in the back door. "Forgot my gardening gloves," he said with a smile. "How's it going?"

Chloe jumped out of her seat. She pointed at Amy. "*She* did it!" Chloe shouted. "She knocked over the water! The cookies are ruined!"

Chapter 6

Fashion Disaster!

Julia and Chloe cleaned up the cookies while Amy helped her dad pull some weeds in the garden.

"Hey, is everything okay, kiddo?" Amy's dad asked her. "You're being awfully quiet."

Amy nodded. But everything *wasn't* okay. *Chloe really doesn't like me,* Amy thought. *Why else would she say I spilled the water?*

"Okay, change of plans!" Julia said, walking outside. Chloe was behind her. "Amy, Chloe and I were talking. How about we three girls go shopping?"

Amy looked at her dad. She gave him her

I-hate-to-shop face. He gave her his *Oh-come-on-it-might-be-fun* face.

"I'll meet you all at the park afterward," her dad said.

"There's a great new bookstore in town," Julia went on. "We could walk there."

"Yeah!" said Chloe. She was smiling. "That's right next to *my* favorite store. We could go to both!"

"Oh!" said Amy. Shopping for books? That *was* fun. *And it kind of seems like Chloe wants me to come.*

"Okay," Amy said. She smiled back at Chloe.

Maybe I was wrong. Maybe she doesn't hate me, after all.

They went to Chloe's favorite store first. It was a clothing store called Threads. As soon as they stepped inside, Chloe disappeared in the clothing racks. Julia waved to the lady at the register. They seemed to know each other. Julia went over to chat.

Amy was left alone. She felt like she was frozen in her spot. It was the

kind of store that made her feel . . . lost. Minutes crept by.

Then Chloe came rushing over. She already had an armload of clothes. "Amy! Come on! Let's try some things on," Chloe said.

"No, that's okay. You can go ahead—" Amy started to say.

But Chloe grabbed her hand. She

pulled Amy to the back of the store. "Look! These would look *so, so good* on you!" Chloe said.

She handed Amy some items on hangers. Then she shooed Amy into a dressing room. "I'll try some things on next door," said Chloe. "Meet out by the mirror in five!"

Before Amy knew it, the door was closed.

Amy sighed. She really didn't

like trying things on in stores! But Chloe was being so nice. How could she say no?

So Amy put on the clothing. She looked at herself in the mirror. *This can't be right,* she thought. *I've heard of mixing patterns like stripes and polka dots. But this is ridiculous. Isn't it?*

Amy thought about
Liz. Her clothes were
colorful and differ-
ent—and she always
got compliments on
her outfits. So maybe
Amy looked okay,
after all.

Amy took a deep breath and
opened the door. Chloe was standing by the mirror. She was wearing
a daisy yellow party dress, purple
ballet flats, and a sparkly head-
band. Her outfit was so pretty!

Amy walked over and stood next

to Chloe. They both looked in the mirror.

In a flash, Amy knew: her outfit was crazy with a capital C.

Then her eyes met Chloe's in the mirror. Amy could see it in Chloe's eyes. *She's trying not to laugh!*

Chloe had made her dress up like a fool.

"Oh, my," said a saleswoman, coming over to Amy. "Dear, *what* are you wearing?"

Amy ran back into the dressing room and closed the door.

Chapter 7

Amy to the Rescue

The trip to the bookstore wasn't much fun either.

At least *Julia* was being nice to Amy, as always. Julia showed Amy her favorite books from when she was a girl. Amy thought she'd like to read some of them.

Then Julia headed to the cook-book section. Chloe came over. "Hey,

Amy," she said. "Have you read these?" She held out a small pile of books. Amy reached out to take them.

Chloe let go before Amy had a grip. The books fell to the floor. *Thwump!* Other shoppers nearby turned to look. Amy's face flushed.

Was it just Amy's imagination, or had Chloe done that on purpose?

In the bookstore café, Julia got each girl a hot chocolate. While Julia paid, Amy headed to the counter. She reached for the cinnamon.

"Oh, I love cinnamon too!" said Chloe, appearing at Amy's side. She snatched up the cinnamon. "Here, let me!" She started sprinkling the cinnamon on Amy's hot chocolate.

"Thanks!" said Amy.

Chloe kept sprinkling.

"Okay!" Amy said. "That's great."

Chloe kept sprinkling.

"Chloe! That's enough!" Amy covered the top of her cup. Chloe finally stopped.

Amy sipped her hot chocolate. It was *way* too cinnamon-y.

Amy was glad when they met her dad in the park. He had brought a picnic for them.

"How was the shopping?" he asked Amy. They were tossing the Frisbee. Chloe and Julia were sitting together over on the picnic blanket.

Amy shrugged. "It—it was okay," she said glumly.

She had thought it would be such a fun weekend. But now she just missed Liz, Ellie, and Marion.

"Call us when you get the good news!" Ellie had said. Turned out it wasn't good news at all. Amy had a wicked stepsister!

Amy threw the Frisbee. The wind blew it a little off course. It glided toward the picnic blanket.

Out of nowhere, a dog came

running out of some bushes. It was chasing the Frisbee and barking like crazy.

Chloe saw the dog coming her way—and let out an ear-piercing scream! She jumped up and darted behind Julia.

Meanwhile, the Frisbee landed next to the blanket. The dog, a Dalmatian, ran right past it. Now the dog was more interested in Chloe! It ran up to her and barked.

Chloe screamed
again and ran behind
a tree.

The dog chased her, barking and
wagging its tail.

Chloe needed help. Amy ran
over. "Chloe," she said calmly. "It's

okay." Chloe looked terrified. "Trust me," Amy said. Then she turned to face the dog. The two girls stood side by side.

"Sit!" Amy said firmly.

The dog stopped barking and froze. Then it sat back on its hind legs.

"Stay!" Amy said.

The dog sat very still, watching Amy. It seemed to be waiting for another command.

Chloe turned to Amy. "Thank you!" she cried, and hugged her tight.

A New Friend?

"Nice going, kiddo," Amy's dad said, and patted her on the back.

Julia had an arm around Chloe, who still looked shaken up. "That was amazing," Julia said. "Thank you, Amy. Chloe is sometimes a little scared of animals."

Amy remembered what Chloe had said earlier about animals

being smelly and dirty. *Maybe she just didn't want to say she was afraid of them.*

"My mom has had Dalmatians at her vet clinic," Amy explained. "She told me that they have a lot of energy and are

very playful. I think this dog just wanted to play with Chloe."

The dog—who was female—was still sitting quietly. She watched them talking.

"She doesn't have a collar or a tag," Amy noticed.

Amy's dad looked around. "I wonder if she got loose from her owner," he said.

Together, they walked around
the park. They didn't see anyone
who seemed to be looking for a dog.

Luckily, the Orange Blossom Animal Shelter was only two blocks away. They decided to take the dog over there. "We can see if anyone has reported her missing," Julia said.

They packed up their picnic basket. As they walked toward the shelter, the dog followed closely behind Amy. Chloe cautiously came up to walk by Amy's side.

"Thanks again, Amy," she said quietly. "You really helped me out."

"It was no problem," Amy said. "Really."

They walked along without talking for a minute. Then Chloe said, "I *was* listening before when you told me about The Critter Club. And that you started it with your three best friends. I have three best friends too. We have a jewelry-making club called the Sapphire Society."

"Cool!" said Amy. "That sounds fun!" She really meant it.

Chloe nodded. "And my mom says you like mysteries?"

Amy beamed. "I wouldn't go anywhere without a Nancy Drew," she told Chloe.

"Me too!" said Chloe.

Wow, thought Amy. *Maybe we do have* some *stuff in common.*

When they got to the Orange Blossom Animal Shelter, they led the dog inside. At the front desk, they met the owner, Mr. Beebe.

"Ah, yes," Mr. Beebe said. "The Dalmatian. I've been getting calls about you, young lady," he said to the dog.

The dog barked once, as if she understood. "I've heard she's been roaming around town for about a week now. We put up some flyers with her description. But we haven't

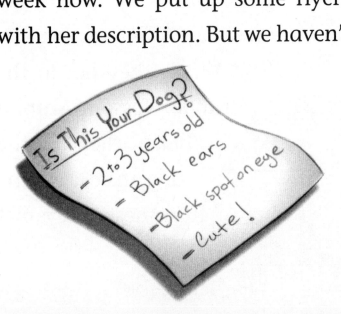

gotten a call from anyone looking for her," Mr. Beebe continued. "She must be a stray."

"Poor girl," said Julia, petting the dog's head. "She seems like she'd make a great pet for someone. What can we do to help her?"

Mr. Beebe sighed. "The problem is, we're pretty crowded right now," he said. "We have so many animals we need to find homes for. I don't suppose you folks know anyone who might be able to find her a good home?"

Amy smiled at her dad. Amy's dad smiled back.

"Mr. Beebe," said Amy, "I know just the place."

A look of understanding brightened Chloe's face. "The Critter Club!" she exclaimed.

Chapter 9

Heart-to-Heart

That evening back at the house, Amy, her dad, Chloe, and Julia were playing a board game.

"It was nice of Mr. Beebe to let Penny stay over tonight at the shelter," said Amy. Penny was the name they'd given the Dalmatian.

Amy's dad nodded. "And it was nice of your mom to agree to pick

Penny up tomorrow when she comes to get you," he said.

Dr. Purvis was even going to give the dog a checkup at her clinic. She wanted to make sure Penny was healthy before they took her to The Critter Club.

"How about some cookies for dessert?" Julia said.

"Yum!" cried Amy and Chloe together. They both laughed.

Amy's dad and Julia went to get the cookies. Chloe rolled the dice.

"You know what?" Chloe said. "I thought of one other thing we have in common."

"What?" said Amy.

"We're both only children," said Chloe. She moved her game piece. "I've always wanted a sister. But when my mom told me that she and your dad were going to get married . . . I don't know. I guess I started to worry about it. I was *super* nervous to meet you."

"Really?" said Amy. "To meet *me*?"

Chloe nodded. "I'm sorry for the way I acted," she said to Amy.

Amy smiled. "That's okay," she told Chloe. "I was really nervous

too. I was scared you wouldn't like me." Her cheeks flushed a little. "And then I was *sure* you didn't."

Chloe shook her head. "No, I just kept messing up! All day! I blamed you for spilling the water because, well, I didn't want your dad to be mad

at me. I just really want him to like me. And at the clothing store, I was trying to be silly, not mean. But then I could tell you were upset and . . . I didn't know what to say."

Amy laughed.

Chloe also explained that she had tripped at the bookstore and accidentally dropped the books. And she hadn't been paying attention with the cinnamon. Chloe looked down. "I'm sorry I messed up your hot chocolate."

"It's really okay," Amy said. She felt so relieved. Her future stepsister wasn't mean, after all. "I guess we

act nervous in different ways. My face turns bright red. You do crazy stuff!"

Amy and Chloe giggled together. Then Amy had an idea.

"You have to come visit me in Santa Vista sometime!" she told Chloe. "I'll take you to The Critter

Club. We have some chicks that are going to hatch soon."

Chloe looked like she was thinking it over. "Chicks?" she said. "You mean like tiny, yellow, fluffy baby chickens?"

Amy nodded. "Yep. They don't bark at all!"

Chloe smiled. "That sounds great. You've got a deal."

More Big, Exciting News

On Sunday, Marion, Ellie, and Liz met Amy at The Critter Club. Amy and her mom had brought Penny over that morning. She seemed to be settling right in. She was already best friends with Rufus, Ms. Sullivan's dog. They ran and played together while Amy told her friends about the weekend. There

was so much to tell: about finding Penny, about her dad getting
engaged, and all about Chloe!

"You guys will like her a lot,"
Amy said. "She likes pretty clothes
and jewelry—just like you, Marion."
Marion smiled. "She decorated her
cookies with lots of cool designs—
like you would, Liz."

"I like her already!" said Liz.

"And she really loves sparkles!" added Amy.

"Like me!" exclaimed Ellie. She twirled around in her sparkly dress. The girls giggled.

"Well, I'm excited to meet her," Marion said. "And I'm glad you're back, Amy."

"Yeah!" said Liz. "We missed you. *And* it's about to get pretty busy around here. Come see!"

She pulled Amy toward the egg incubator inside the barn. Amy gasped. There was a teeny, tiny beak poking out of a hole in one of the eggs.

"Surprise!" Ellie said.

"It started hatching yesterday," said Marion, "ahead of schedule."

"The others can't be far behind!" Liz added.

Amy clapped. "Amazing!" she exclaimed. She looked at the little chick peeking out at them. "You're the very first one! But your new brothers and sisters could hatch any minute now!"

Then Amy leaned in closer. She whispered something only the chick could hear: "Don't be nervous. I'm sure you guys will get along great."

the CRitteR club

Liz at Marigold Lake

Table of Contents

Chapter 1

Sleepover at the Lake!

Squee-onk! Squee-onk! A loud, shrill sound woke Liz Jenkins. *My alarm clock sounds broken,* she thought, only half-awake.

Liz rolled over in bed and rubbed her eyes. No, it wasn't her alarm clock. It was a goose honking! Sunlight shone in through the window. Birds chirped outside. It was going to be a beautiful spring day at the cabin.

Liz threw off her flannel sheets and jumped out of bed. "Yes!" she cheered. "It's the perfect weather for the girls' visit!"

Liz's three best friends, Ellie, Marion, and Amy, were coming up to the Jenkins' lake cabin *today* for the three-day weekend. For years, they had heard all about it from Liz. She and her family had been coming to Marigold Lake since Liz was little. But this was the first time Liz had been able to invite her friends.

Liz hurried to change into her clothes. She had lots of things to get ready before the girls arrived. She

wanted their first visit to the lake to be perfect.

Out in the cabin's living room, Liz's mom, dad, and big brother, Stewart, were already up. Her dad was making breakfast. Her mom

was sweeping up pine needles from the floor. Stewart was setting the table.

"Oatmeal in ten minutes, Lizzie!" her dad said.

"Thanks, Dad," Liz replied. She was headed for the door. "I'll be back. I just need to do a few things."

Outside, Liz took a deep breath. *Ahhhh.* Fresh air. She

smiled at the sight of the big, beautiful lake in the cabin's backyard.

Liz went into the storage shed. She dragged a folded-up tent to a flat area by the campfire pit. "Just the spot," Liz said out loud to herself. She would ask her mom or dad to help her set up the tent later. It

was definitely warm enough for the girls to sleep outside in it. Liz couldn't wait to surprise them!

Next, Liz hurried down to the boat dock. She took the tarp off the red canoe and made sure the life jackets were there. *We can paddle around the whole lake,* she thought.

Then, on her way back to the cabin, Liz picked up every long, thin stick she saw. *We're* definitely *roasting marshmallows over a campfire*, she decided. She left her pile of roasting sticks next to the campfire pit.

Liz stopped to think. Canoeing, swimming, camping out, marshmallow-roasting, plus hiking on the nature path . . .

I hope we have time for everything! she thought excitedly.

Back inside the cabin, Liz joined

her family at the table. They had already served her oatmeal and yogurt—their usual super-healthy breakfast. Her dad passed her some berries to sprinkle on top while Liz told them about her preparations.

Liz's parents smiled. "Sounds like you've thought of everything," her mom said.

Then Stewart added, "But won't you guys just be painting your nails and stuff? Or whatever you do at your sleepovers?"

Liz rolled her eyes at her brother.

"*Actually*, my friends are so excited to have a wilderness weekend. I told them about all the animals up here—the rabbits, squirrels, deer, and foxes."

Liz and her friends were different in lots of ways, but they all shared one thing: a love of animals. Together they ran an animal shelter called The Critter Club in their town of Santa Vista. They helped all kinds of stray and hurt animals.

"You told them about *all* the animals we've seen?" Stewart asked. "Like the snakes? And the bear we saw that one time?"

Liz hadn't exactly mentioned *those*. Her friends weren't as excited as Liz was about unusual animals. Like the cool pet tarantula they

took care of at The Critter Club over the summer. Ellie, Marion, and

Amy were glad Liz wanted to be in charge of it.

Liz shrugged and ate her oatmeal. *My friends will love the lake as much as I do!* she thought. *Or almost as much. Or at least they'll like it a lot.*

Chapter 2

Welcome to the Wilderness!

Ellie's mom's van pulled up to the cabin just after lunchtime.

"Liz!" Ellie cried, jumping out of the back of the van. "Oh, we have missed you!"

Amy and Marion jumped out behind her. Marion giggled. "We just saw her *yesterday* at school," she reminded Ellie.

"I know!" said Ellie. "But so much has happened since then."

Liz and her family had driven to the lake the day before—on Friday afternoon. So Liz had missed the girls' after-school duties at The Critter Club.

"Don't worry, Liz," Marion said. "We'll get you all caught up."

The four girls huddled for a group hug. "I'm so glad you're here!" Liz told them. "Now the fun can begin!"

They said goodbye to Ellie's mom. Then Liz led her friends

down to the lake. They sat on the boat dock. There the girls told Liz the latest Critter Club news.

"First of all," said Amy, "our stray isn't a stray anymore."

Liz gasped. The girls had been taking care of a stray cat for a few weeks. "She's been adopted?" Liz asked.

"Even better," said Ellie. "Her owner called! He saw the ad you drew for the newspaper, Liz. Oh I brought a copy."

Liz's family didn't get the paper at their cabin, so she was excited to see her art in print.

Stray Cat Found!
Gray female with white patches.
Sweet, gentle, very healthy

Can you give her a home?
Call The Critter Club!

"It was so sweet," said Marion. "The cat saw him and jumped right into his arms."

"Oh! And Grandma Sue stopped by yesterday," Ellie added.

Grandma Sue wasn't Ellie's grandmother. The girls just called her that. They had met her when they delivered a singing telegram to her from her grandchildren.

"She came with her new love-bird, Princess Two," Ellie went on. "Princess Two and Princess Boo are already best friends."

The girls had helped Grandma Sue when Princess Boo was acting

strangely. With the help of Amy's mom, a veterinarian, they figured out the bird wasn't sick—she was just lonely. That's why Grandma Sue had gotten a second bird.

"Oh, I'm sad I missed the chance to meet her," Liz said. But she shook off her disappointment. Her friends were here and they had the whole weekend ahead of them. "Let me show you guys around."

The other girls jumped up, ready to follow their tour guide.

Liz took them to the cabin. She pointed out the solar panels up on the roof. "All of our hot water is heated by the sun," Liz said.

She showed them the outdoor shower. "You can rinse off here after a swim in the lake," she explained.

Liz took them inside. She showed them the shelves full of books and board games next to the fireplace.

Finally, Liz showed the girls her room.

"This is so great, Liz!" Ellie exclaimed.

"Yeah," said Amy. "No wonder you love it up here."

Marion was looking around Liz's room. "I *love* your room," she said.

"But there's only one bed in here. Where will *we* sleep?"

Liz's eyes lit up. "I'm glad you asked," she said. "Follow me."

Liz led the way back down

toward the lake. She stopped next to the campfire pit. "Ta-da!" she said, presenting the tent. Her dad had already set it up for them. "We can sleep here tonight. Won't that be the best?"

Liz looked at her friends' faces. Amy looked kind of excited. Ellie looked curious.

Marion looked worried. She glanced at Liz. She glanced at the tent. Then she glanced at Liz again. "You mean we're going to sleep . . . *outside?*" she said.

Chapter 3

Shivers and Jitters

"Last one to the floating platform is a rotten egg!" Liz shouted. She dove off the boat dock into the lake. She swam toward the platform. When she came up for air, she looked around.

Where were her friends?

Liz looked back at the boat dock. Marion was shivering, wrapped in

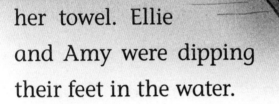

her towel. Ellie
and Amy were dipping
their feet in the water.

Ellie called out to Liz: "It's kind
of cold, isn't it?"

"Not really!" Liz called back.
"Just jump! It's great once you're in
the lake!"

But the girls didn't look so sure.
So Liz swam back to them.

Liz climbed out onto the boat dock. "I have an idea," she said to them. "Let's hold hands. On the count of three, we all jump in together. Okay?"

The girls looked at each other. One by one, they each nodded.

"One, two, three . . ."

They all jumped in with a *splash*!
When her head popped up, Amy
squealed loudly: "Eeeeeeek!"

"It's freeeeeeeeezing!" exclaimed
Ellie, half-laughing.

"Ohhmygosh, ohhmygosh," said
Marion, treading water.

"Keep swimming! Follow me!"

called Liz. "You'll warm up. I promise!"

The girls played Marco Polo and swimming tag. Soon they were having a blast. They floated on their backs and looked for pictures in the clouds. They talked while blowing bubbles in the water, seeing if each other could understand.

They were all laughing when they climbed onto the floating platform in the middle of the lake. The sun-warmed wooden planks felt nice as the girls stretched out to rest.

Then the breeze picked up. Before long, Marion, Ellie, and Amy were shivering.

"I think I'm r-r-ready to go in," Marion said. Her teeth chattered.

"Oh," said Liz, "okay." She had hoped they could spend a while doing silly jumps off the platform. But she didn't want her friends to be cold. So they swam back to shore.

Back on land, the girls changed into dry clothes. Liz's dad offered to take them on a nature walk.

"We can collect cool leaves," Liz suggested. "Then I'll show you how to make some fun leaf prints."

Ellie smiled. "Nature plus art," she said. "Sounds like Liz, all right!"

The girls laughed as they followed Liz's dad toward the nature trail. Stewart waved from the cabin porch. "Have fun! Watch out for snakes!" he called.

Ellie stopped in her tracks. *"Snakes?"* she said, her eyes wide with fear. "What snakes?"

Chapter 4

A Very Short Walk

It took a while for Liz and her dad to reassure Ellie.

"We've never seen any *poisonous* snakes," Liz pointed out.

"That's right," said Mr. Jenkins. "And in *all* the years we've come to the lake, we've only seen a few snakes total."

Liz could tell Ellie wasn't so into

the nature walk anymore. But Ellie finally agreed to come along. "I want to walk in the middle of the group—not up front, not in the back," she said.

The nature trail went all the way around the lake. It was a walk that usually took Liz about an hour.

Just ten minutes down the trail, Liz, Marion, and Amy already had handfuls of leaves. Ellie was too busy watching for snakes to look for leaves.

"Here's my favorite so far," said Liz, holding up an oak leaf.

"I like this one!" said Amy.

"Oooh, birch!" said Liz. She knew a thing or two about the trees around the lake.

Marion held one up. "How about this one?" she asked

"Maple, for sure, Liz replied. "So pretty!"

Ellie sighed. "Oh,

I'm being ridiculous!" she said. "I want to find a special leaf too." She took one step off the trail, reaching down for a leaf. Her foot came down on the very end of a long stick. The other end popped up from underneath a pile of leaves.

Ellie jumped up and screamed. "Aaaaaaah! Snaaaaaaaake!" She took off, running back toward the cabin.

Liz's heart sank. Poor Ellie! It seemed the nature walk was over.

Chapter 5

Row, Row, Row Your Boat

Back at the cabin, Stewart was very sorry when he saw how upset Ellie was. After all, he was the one who had put the idea of snakes in her head. To make it up to the girls, he offered to take them on a canoe ride. "I'll row the row boat," Stewart said. "You guys ride in the canoe. We can tie the two together and I'll tow you around the lake."

Ellie cheered up right away. "That sounds fun!" she said, beaming at Stewart. "But could I ride with *you*?"

Stewart shrugged. "If you want," he said.

The five of them put on life

jackets. Then Stewart tied a rope line from the back of the row boat to the front of the canoe.

Soon Stewart was rowing them out into the middle of the lake. In

the canoe, Marion, Amy, and Liz
lounged and relaxed.

"I could get used to this," Marion
said.

"Me too," said Liz. "Stewart has
never, *ever* rowed me around the
lake before."

The late-afternoon sun was getting low in the sky. The water on the lake was still, except for the pools made by Stewart's oars. Liz sighed. It was a peaceful, happy, perfect moment.

Just then, on the far side of the

lake, a very large bird came splashing down to the water as it landed. Amy gasped. "Wow!" she cried. "Is that a great blue heron?" She leaped to her feet, straining to see.

"Wait!" cried Liz. "Don't stand—"

It was too late. Amy teetered, then lost her balance. She fell out of the canoe, her foot catching the side. The whole canoe flipped, dumping Marion and Liz too.

When Liz came up from under the water, the first thing she heard

was Stewart laughing. But Liz didn't mind. She started laughing too. Liz had lost track of the number of times she and Stewart had tipped the canoe over the years.

Marion started giggling too. "Good thing I brought an extra pair of shoes!" she said.

"Are you guys okay?" Ellie called from the row boat. Liz could tell Ellie was trying not to laugh at her wet friends.

The only one who did not look amused was Amy. Liz recognized the familiar flush of pink on her cheeks.

Amy was completely embarrassed.

Chapter 6

The Campout

Inside the cozy cabin, a warm fire crackled in the fireplace. Liz sat at the table, watching her family and friends chatting happily. Her parents had made them all a big dinner.

But Liz was feeling blue—and not very hungry. She loved grilled tofu and beet salad and roasted organic sweet potatoes. But did her mom have to make it this week-end? *Couldn't we have spaghetti, or something I know my friends like?* she thought.

Ellie was mostly pushing the tofu around on her plate. Marion hadn't touched the beets. Amy was chewing slowly and taking lots of sips of water.

After dinner, the girls settled into

the tent. Their four sleeping bags fit inside perfectly. Liz's mom found extra flashlights so each of them could have one. Then she zipped the tent flap closed.

"Good night, girls," she said through the nylon. "Don't stay up too late."

In the flashlight glow, the girls crawled into their sleeping bags.

"Marion," said Ellie, "did you bring your notebook?"

"Of course!" Marion replied, pulling it out of her backpack. Marion was super organized. She

loved making lists, so she always had paper and a pen.

"Great!" Ellie exclaimed. "We can play Two Truths and a Lie."

"Oh yeah," Amy said. "That game we played last weekend at our sleepover!"

The girls took turns hosting a sleepover nearly every Friday night, so they knew a lot of sleepover games. To play Two Truths and a Lie, each girl got a slip of paper. She wrote down two things about herself that were true and one that was not. Then the others had to figure out which one was the lie.

Liz stared at her paper, thinking. Then she wrote:

| I love grilled tofu. |
| I once swam all the way across the lake. |
| |

Then she added:

| I am having a bad weekend. |

The last one should have been a lie, but it was actually the truth. Liz knew Marion didn't even want to sleep out here. Poor Ellie was freaked out by the snake-stick. And Amy was still embarrassed about tipping the canoe. Plus the lake was too cold for them, and the food was too weird.

Liz sighed. She crossed out her last sentence and tried to think of a different one—one that really *was* a lie.

Chapter 7

Some Squeaky Guests

Everything looks a little brighter with the sun, Liz thought the next morning. That's what her mom always said. She unzipped the tent flap and peeked outside. It was a new day. Liz was ready to leave yesterday's troubles behind.

"Sleeping out here was so fun!" Amy said. They were walking up to

the cabin for breakfast.

"Yeah!" said Ellie. "Can we do it again tonight?"

Liz nodded. She noticed Marion wasn't saying anything, but she tried not to worry about it.

On the porch, they passed the leaf prints they had made the day before.

"They're dry," Liz announced.

"They look so good!" Marion said, holding hers up.

"They really do," Amy agreed.

"Liz," said Ellie, "you've made us all artists!"

Liz smiled a huge smile. The prints *had* turned out beautifully. More important, her friends had fun making them. Maybe Ellie's snake-stick scare had been worth it after all.

Inside, the girls found Liz's parents huddled over a cardboard box on the kitchen counter.

"Oh girls," Mrs. Jenkins said, "are we glad you're here!"

Liz and her friends looked at one another, puzzled. "What's going on?" Liz asked.

"Well," Mr. Jenkins explained, "last night we heard some noises."

Liz's mom nodded. "Little tiny squeaks. Coming from somewhere inside the cabin. And this morning, we found what was making them."

She nodded toward the box. The girls came over to look inside—and gasped.

"Awwwwww," Liz cooed.

"They're adorable!" cried Ellie.

Cuddled together on a kitchen towel at the bottom of the box were a bunch of tiny animals. They were covered in a light brown fuzz. They

had long, skinny, pink tails and rounded ears. Their eyes were shut tight.

"Baby mice?" Amy asked.

Liz's dad nodded. "Yep! We found them in the back corner of

the pantry closet. There was a little nest too. But we can't find any sign of the mother."

"They looked so cold in there," Liz's mom added. "We thought they might be more comfortable in this box. There's a hot water bottle under the towel to keep them warm."

"What if the mother comes back?" Amy asked. "She won't be able to find them."

"Oh, no! She'll be so worried!" Ellie said dramatically.

The girls thought for a minute. Liz's eyes lit up. "I have an idea!" she cried.

Liz got some scissors from a kitchen drawer. Carefully, she cut out a mouse-size hole on one side of the cardboard box. "A door for Mama Mouse," she explained.

Then Liz carried the box to the

pantry closet. She laid it gently in the back corner. "Now they're snug and comfy, but if their mom comes back, she can find them."

Liz's friends and parents agreed: it was the perfect solution. Liz felt very proud!

"There's just one more thing," said Ellie. "What if the mother *doesn't* come back?"

Chapter 8

Critter Sitters

The girls knew one person who was sure to have some answers: Amy's mom, Dr. Melanie Purvis.

Amy used the cabin phone to call her mom back in Santa Vista. Marion sat next to her. She took notes in her notebook to help Amy remember everything her mom told them.

"So?" said Ellie the moment Amy hung up the phone. "What did your mom say?"

Amy sat down in front of the fireplace. The girls gathered around, eager to hear all the info.

"Mom thinks they're probably about two weeks old," Amy said.

"And what did she say about the mother mouse?" Liz asked.

"Well," said Amy, "here's the bad news: she said if it's been more than a couple of hours, the mother probably isn't coming back."

Liz, Marion, and Ellie looked

at one another, not knowing what they could do.

"But there's good news," Amy said. "We can take care of them. They'll need our help to eat for a few weeks."

Huge grins spread across the girls' faces.

"The Critter Club's work is never done!" Liz exclaimed.

Marion showed them her notes. She had made a list of supplies they needed to take care of the mice.

Kitten or puppy formula (replacement milk)

Eyedropper →

Water bottle (like for a hamster)

Liz's dad offered to go shopping. "There's a pet supply store in town," he said. "I'll run out and get what you need."

"In the meantime," Liz's mom said, "why don't you girls head down to the lake? I packed you a picnic breakfast." She held up a basket filled with muffins and fruit. "And I'll keep my eye on the mice for you."

The girls thanked Liz's parents. Liz took the basket and led the way down to the boat dock.

"So what should we do today?" Liz asked the girls as they nibbled on blueberry oat bran muffins. "There's a cool waterfall in the woods I could take you to."

Ellie frowned. "In the woods?" she asked. "How far into the woods?"

Liz sighed. *Oh right*, she thought. *Ellie's still nervous about the snakes.*

"Ah-CHOO!" Marion sneezed a huge sneeze.

"Bless you!" Liz, Ellie, and Amy said all together.

Marion sniffled. "Thank y—ah-CHOOOO!" She sneezed even louder and rubbed her eyes. "Uh-oh."

"What's the matter?" Liz asked.

"I just hope I'm not getting sick," Marion replied. "You know, from the chilly lake yesterday. I have a horse show next week that I do *not* want to miss. Maybe I'd better not swim today."

Marion rode her horse, Coco,

in all kinds of competitions. Sometimes they even won ribbons. Liz hated to think the trip to the lake had made Marion sick.

"And I guess I'd better stay out of the canoe," Amy said. "I don't want to dunk anyone again!" She said it with a half laugh. But Liz ᴵdered if Amy still ᵉlt bad about the whole thing.

Liz turned her head away from the girls. She stared out at the lake. Her vision was getting blurry as her eyes filled with tears. She bit her lip, trying hard not to cry.

They hate it here, Liz thought.

Swimming is out. Canoeing is out. Hiking to the waterfall is out.

"Should we just take the baby mice and head back to Santa Vista today—a day early?" Liz asked them.

With the words out, she couldn't hold back the sobs anymore. Liz covered her face, turned, and ran off the boat dock.

Chapter 9

Friends to the Rescue

"Can we come up?" Ellie asked.

She, Marion, and Amy craned their necks, looking up at Liz. She was in a tree, about ten feet off the ground.

Liz nodded. "Yeah, sure." She sniffed. She wiped her eyes. She'd let it all out. Now she was feeling better—although maybe a little silly.

"Actually," Ellie called up, "can you come down?"

Liz looked down. The girls were having trouble climbing the tree. She couldn't help laughing through her sniffles. She had forgotten that

it took her one whole summer to figure out how to get up into that tree!

With a few quick moves, Liz was
back on the ground. "I'm sorry, you
guys," she said. "I just . . . I just had
all these ideas about how this weekend would be. I wanted you to have

a great time. I guess I didn't realize how much I wanted it."

Her friends moved in. They all wrapped their arms around Liz. Liz put her head on Ellie's shoulder.

"You don't have to say sorry for

being sad," Ellie said. "We're your best friends!"

"She's right," said Amy. "Friends should be honest about their feelings."

Marion nodded. "So we'll be honest," she said. "We *are* having a great time."

Liz looked up at them. "You are?" she asked. *"Really?"*

All three of them smiled and nodded. "Really!" they said together.

"But . . . but . . . ," Liz began.

She listed all the things that hadn't gone as planned: the snake-stick, the flipped canoe, the water that was too cold for them. "Nobody feels like swimming or canoeing," she added. "And now Marion might be getting sick."

Marion gave Liz a squeeze. "Oh, don't worry about that," she said. "I'll be fine. I just need to eat more of your mom's veggies, I guess."

"And yesterday was *so fun!*" said Amy. "We had a blast swimming— before we got chilly. Even canoe-ing was great." She giggled. "I can actually laugh about it now."

Ellie chimed in. "It makes a good story, that's for sure," she said. "And I know there's no reason to be afraid of a little snake. I'm in The Critter Club, after all!"

Ellie stood up straight and tall.

"So it's decided," she went on. "You're taking us to that waterfall. The one deep, deep in the woods. The deeper, the better!"

The girls laughed together.

"Aw, thanks, you guys," Liz said. "I feel so much better. You really are the best friends in the world."

"You too, Liz," said Marion. "And you're the world's best wilderness guide. So lead the way!"

Chapter 10

Campfire Chat

That night, around a glowing campfire, the girls roasted marsh- mallows with the sticks Liz had col- lected. Liz turned her stick slowly so her marshmallow cooked evenly all around.

Then, as they ate their treats, they talked about the day.

"My favorite part was the

waterfall, for sure," said Ellie. "I'm so glad I braved the evil snake-stick to see it."

"Well, my favorite was canoe-ing," Amy said. "I didn't even flip it *one time* today."

Marion put another marshmal-low on her stick. "I think my favorite part of the day is still to come," she said. "You're not going to believe it: it's sleeping outside in the tent!"

"*Really?*" the girls said.

Marion nodded. "I've never done it before this weekend," she explained. "But I really like it. Being

out in the cool air, bundled up in a cozy warm sleeping bag, plus the sound of the crickets all around . . . It's the best!"

Liz gave a happy little clap. "Well, that does it," she said. "I think *this* is my favorite part." Hearing what her friends loved about the lake made her day. Then she had another thought. "This *and* taking care of the mice. They are just so cute. And they need us so much."

The mother mouse had not returned. So every few hours that day, the girls had fed the babies, with the help of Liz's parents. They used the special milk Liz's dad bought at the pet supply store. They dripped drops of it into the babies' tiny mouths.

"My mom says we have a tough decision ahead," Amy said. "After we bring them to The Critter Club, when the baby mice are bigger, they could be released back into the wild. They are wild animals, after all. Or we could try to find homes

for them as pets."

Liz wasn't sure what the right thing to do was. "If we let them go, would they be okay?" she asked.

Amy shrugged. "It's hard to say," she said. "We would need to help them get ready. My mom says there's a special kind of mouse

house we could build for them. It would help them get used to living outside on their own."

Liz stared into the campfire. The flames jumped and danced. "It's funny," Liz said. "Tomorrow our wilderness weekend is over. But it turns out we'll be taking some of the wilderness home with us!"

It sounded like The Critter Club girls were going to have their hands full with the mice for a little while. Liz knew they'd figure out the right thing to do—together.

"So . . . , " Liz said slowly, "do you guys want to do another trip to the lake sometime?"

"*Yes!*" Ellie, Marion, and Amy all replied at the same time—and Liz knew they really meant it.

Read on for a sneak peek at
the next Critter Club book:

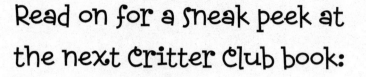

#8

Marion Strikes a Pose

Marion walked in the front door of Santa Vista Elementary School. In her head, she was going through her morning checklist: *Homework folder? Check. Lunch box? Check. Sneakers for gym? Check.*

Marion felt ready for the day.

She followed other kids into the auditorium for the morning assembly, which they had every

Friday. The seats were filling up. Marion headed for the rows assigned to the second-grade classes. She spotted an empty seat next to her three best friends, Amy, Liz, and Ellie.

Walking toward that row, Marion passed a group of fourth graders. "I love your skirt, Marion!" said a girl named Emily as Marion went by.

"Thanks!" Marion replied. She had spent a lot of time last night planning her outfit for today. She added one more item to her checklist.

Cool outfit? Check! Marion loved picking out her outfits for school. And for play dates and for parties. And for riding her horse, Coco. For everything, really!

"Hi, Marion!" said Amy as she sat down. Farther down the row, Ellie and Liz waved.

"Attention, students!" Mrs. Young, the principal, spoke into the microphone at the front of the auditorium. All the kids quieted down. "I have some announcements. But first, we have a special guest. Her name is Hannah Lewis. She is the owner of The Closet, a store here in Santa Vista."

The students clapped.

Marion gasped. *The Closet!* It was her absolute favorite clothing store.

Marion sat up straight in her seat as Hannah Lewis walked up to the microphone. Marion loved Hannah's outfit—an extra-long top with a leather belt, black leggings, and ballet flats. Plus she had on some cool beaded necklaces.

"Good morning, everyone," said Hannah. "Thank you, Mrs. Young, for letting me come today. I want to announce that we will be having a special fashion show at The Closet in a few weeks."

A fashion show, Marion thought. *How fun!*

"The purpose of the show is to raise money for a charity," said Hannah. "It provides free clothing to children who need it, so it's a very good cause. We hope the fashion show will get lots of people to come shopping at our store that day. All the money we earn will go to the charity."

"What a great idea," whispered Marion. Amy gave a thumbs-up in agreement.

"But I need *your* help," Hannah went on. "Our store is a *kids'* clothing store. And I was thinking: Who knows best what kids like to wear? Kids! So I am looking for some young fashion designers."

Marion's eyes went wide. This was just getting better and better!

"The Closet is having a styling contest," Hannah explained. "To enter, you style an outfit—head to toe. I will pick one winning look from each grade. Those will be the outfits in our fashion show!"

Now Marion was so excited she could hardly sit still!

"Contest entries are due a week from Monday," Hannah went on. "I have flyers here with all the rules. If you are interested, please come up to get one."

Marion jumped out of her seat, ready to get a flyer.

Seeing Marion, Hannah laughed. "*After* assembly," she added. "But I like your enthusiasm."

Marion sat back down, too

excited to even be embarrassed. She felt as if this contest had been made just for her.

I have to win! she thought. *I just have to!*

Froggy Fashion Show

After school, the girls met at The Critter Club. That was the animal shelter they had started in their friend Ms. Sullivan's empty barn. At the club, they took care of stray and hurt animals and tried to find homes for them.

They also did a lot of pet sitting. Right now at The Critter Club they were taking care of some frogs for a family that was on vacation. It was Liz and Marion's turn to check on the frogs, but Amy and Ellie had come, too. It was fun to all be there together.

Always organized, Marion pulled the frog feeding schedule from her backpack. "I guess it's my day to feed them," she said. "But, do you want to do it, Liz?"

"Yes!" Liz cried excitedly. For Liz, the more unusual the animal, the better. Turtles, snakes, spiders—she loved them all.

Marion shivered. The frogs were not exactly *her* favorite Critter Club guests. They looked so slimy. And they ate bugs. Yuck!

While Liz fed the frogs, Marion pulled the contest flyer out of her backpack. She hadn't stopped thinking about it since assembly.

The Closet's Styling Contest!

Style a head-to-toe outfit for a girl or boy.

Use your own clothes or come "shop" at The Closet to borrow clothes for your outfit design!

"Are you going to enter?" Marion asked her friends.

Amy shook her head no. "Maybe if it was a writing contest," she said with a smile.

Liz also shook her head. "I don't know how to *design* an outfit. Mine just kind of happen."

"What about you, Ellie?" Marion asked. Ellie loved dressing up.

Ellie twirled around and then curtsied. "I'd rather be *on* the stage than styling *back*stage." she replied.

The girls all laughed. That was Ellie, all right! She loved being in the spotlight.

"Well, I have a favor to ask of you guys," Marion said. "I stopped at home and picked out an outfit for each of you from my closet. You know, to get my styling ideas started."

Marion pulled out the clothes she'd brought. "I thought we could play Fashion Show. Right here in the barn!"

Marion had brought a sparkly skirt and satin blouse for Ellie.

"Cuuuuute!" Ellie cooed. She rushed into a storage room to try them on. She was back in less than a minute.

"Ta-da!" Ellie said, striking a pose. Marion added a beaded silk flower to her hair. "Oh, this is *so* me!"

Marion smiled and pulled out Amy's outfit. It was a striped yellow T-shirt dress.

"Would you try it on?" Marion asked Amy. *"Please?"*

Amy didn't look so sure about the fashion show idea, but she agreed. She went off to change and came back, all smiles.

"This is *definitely* something I would wear," Amy said.

Finally, Marion had a colorful outfit for Liz: a bright green dress and rainbow-striped leggings.

Liz had just taken the lid off the frog tank to feed the frogs, but she glanced over. When she saw the outfit, she clapped happily. "I can't wait to try that on! You really know our styles!"

"Thanks, Liz." Marion said. "That's so nice to—EEEEEK!"

Marion shrieked as a frog jumped out of the tank.

The frog landed on the table.

"I'll get it!" said Amy. "Oh, wait! We're not supposed to touch them." Amy grabbed a butterfly net. She tried to catch the frog but it quickly hopped away. "Hey, come back here!" she cried.

The frog hopped onto the outfit Marion had brought for Liz.

"Shoo! Shoo!" Marion cried. The slimy frog was hopping all over the clothes! "Somebody get it off!"

Finally, Amy scooped up the frog in the net. She gently put it back into the frog tank. Marion took a deep breath. Liz, Amy, and Ellie turned to look at her.

Then all four girls burst out laughing.

"You know, Marion," said Liz, "frogs are really cool in lots of ways."

Amy nodded. "My mom is going to come next week. She can teach us more about them."

Amy's mom, Dr. Melanie Purvis, was a veterinarian. She often helped the girls care for the animals at The Critter Club. "Who knows? Maybe you'll even learn to like them."

Marion smiled and didn't say anything. *I wouldn't count on that!* she thought.

A Wrinkle in the Plan

"What a great idea!" said Liz. She was looking at the stack of cards Marion had made over the weekend. Each one had a photo of an item of clothing Marion owned.

"I call them style cards," Marion said as Liz handed them back. "I can carry them around and flip through them to get design ideas."

It was Monday and their class was in the art room. Liz and Marion sat across from each other at one end of a long table. Today they were painting with watercolors.

Marion had carefully painted a few lines, but most of her paper was empty. She didn't love painting. Paintbrushes didn't have erasers. What if she messed up?

Next to Marion, a girl named Olivia leaned over. "Marion," she said, "could *I* look at those?" She pointed at the stack of style cards.

"Sure!" Marion replied. She

handed the cards to Olivia.

Olivia studied them carefully, looking very interested. "You always wear the coolest outfits," she told Marion.

Marion smiled. "Thanks!" she exclaimed.

Olivia nodded and went back to flipping through the cards.

Marion was surprised by the compliment. She had never really noticed Olivia's taste in clothes before. Today Olivia was wearing a purple sweater with a crooked heart on it, black jeans, and purple high-top sneakers. It seemed like their styles were really different.

Olivia passed the cards back. "Thanks for letting me look," she said, and gave Marion a friendly smile. Marion smiled back.

"Could I ask you a favor?" Olivia asked her.

Marion nodded. "Sure."

"Well, I was wondering . . ." Olivia began. She looked unsure of her words. "Could you maybe, I don't know, give *me* some fashion tips sometime?"

Marion was so flattered. She and

Olivia were friendly, but they didn't know each other super well. *She must really like my fashion sense to ask me for advice*, Marion thought.

Marion smiled. "Sure!" she told Olivia.

"Thanks!" Olivia exclaimed happily. "Maybe now I'll have a shot at winning."

Marion was confused. "Winning?" she asked.

Olivia nodded. "Winning the styling contest," Olivia explained. "I'm entering, too."

"Oh." It was all Marion could

think of to say. But her mind was racing. She and Olivia were both in second grade. Hannah would choose only one winning look from each grade. So if Olivia was entering, and Marion was entering, that meant . . .

Olivia was her competition.

And Marion had just agreed to help her win.

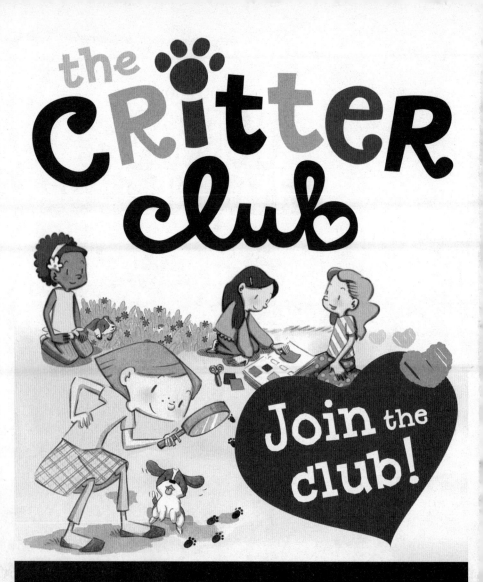

the CRITTER club

Join the club!